THERE'S A
PERSON IN HERE

THERE'S A
PERSON IN HERE

THERE'S A PERSON IN HERE

A Collection of Short Stories and Poems About Holding On, Letting Go, and the Space In-Between

JAMES PATRICK

ARCHWAY
PUBLISHING

Archway Publishing books may be ordered through booksellers or by contacting:

Archway Publishing
1663 Liberty Drive
Bloomington, IN 47403
www.archwaypublishing.com
1-(888)-242-5904

ISBN: 978-1-4808-0737-2 (sc)
ISBN: 978-1-4808-0738-9 (e)

Library of Congress Control Number: 2014907864

Printed in the United States of America

Archway Publishing rev. date: 12/29/14

DEDICATION

This work is dedicated to my entire family ...everyone living
now, and the so many before, with the deepest gratitude for the
time spent, the memories provided, and the acceptance given.

Much credit, appreciation, and love is also given
to my late son, Patrick Dixon, whose continued
presence has helped co-author this work.

CONTENTS

ACKNOWLEDGMENTS

A special thank you is long overdue to those I bother the most:

My wife, Valerie, for everything she does, which is everything.
My children, Maggie, Molly, and Bryan, who are my religion.
Norma and Jim, my late mother and father, for all they
taught me, with an apology for all I misunderstood.
My brothers, William and Kevin, for standing by me, even in my absence.
My Uncle Jack, the man who taught me by
example how to make my father smile.

And,

Mae and Bill, Grace and Jim, Kitty and Phil, Joe, Mr. D, Billy and
MaryAnn, Mary and Tony, Jayne, Father John and Father Henry,
William, Gordon and Mae, Terry, Ruth, Linda, John, Gert, Winnie, Hattie,
Mr. Hattie, Webster, Little Steve, Big Steve, Ellen, David, Scott, Sam and
Sam, Billy and Jimmy, Frank, Peggy, George, Jimmy, Danny, Larry, Steve,
Peggy H. (and Kippy) as well as others I may have forgotten to mention.

And finally,

Dr. Norman Straker, whose ears heard what mine could
not and whose eyes saw what mine would not.

PREFACE

If you want ...you can see inside me now ...

From so far away ...

You can know now ...what I did not know then ...

I RUN THIS

I run
This movie
All day long
Scenes of then
Scenes of now
Joy
Children
Life
Death
Birth
Scenes
Of yesterday
And long ago
Loops of the lost
Laughing with
The projections
Of the living
Clips of memories
Rushing
Toward today
Mixing with
Clips from now
To create
Another tomorrow
I run
This movie
Forward and back
Slowly and quickly
I run
This movie
Without a pause button
Longing
For a freeze-frame

100 THOUGHTS

1. No dinner that night either but
2. It didn't start out that way
3. Was it July, August, September?
4. By October he was too sick
5. So earlier then
6. When I went to visit
7. The man alone
8. Perhaps
9. For the first time
10. Both the visit
11. And his aloneness
12. He had been apart before
13. Maybe half the time
14. But never alone
15. Not this way
16. She was dead
17. Since May
18. He was in shock
19. But didn't realize that then
20. Did anyone?
21. That is another story
22. He seemed slower
23. More distant than ever
24. I waited in the living room
25. For a while
26. I imagined
27. I knew
28. What he was thinking
29. Could I?
30. Regret?
31. Emptiness?
32. Silence?

33. Who to talk to?
34. She was gone to all who knew her
35. And a young sixty-two
36. And fast
37. Faster than him
38. He was probably thinking that too
39. So fast and before himself
40. He did not expect it
41. Never saw it coming
42. Who could have?
43. She cared for him
44. In so many ways
45. For so very long
46. Especially the last years
47. In and out of the hospital
48. For various reasons
49. And various transfusions
50. Had he treated her well?
51. Was he fair?
52. Did he miss her?
53. Diamonds at Christmas
54. Regrets after death
55. What flashed before him?
56. As he now moved around their half-empty bedroom
57. What did he see?
58. Her high school smile?
59. The honeymoon?
60. Her joys?
61. Her disappointments?
62. Her forgiving looks?
63. I waited for him in the living room
64. For too long
65. When I went to his bedroom
66. He was puttering
67. He was not a putterer
68. When I went to his bedroom
69. He was weak

70. He was never weak
71. When I went to his bedroom
72. He was sad
73. He was never sad
74. At least that I knew
75. Mad
76. On occasion
77. Never sad
78. I don't remember how I left
79. Or when
80. But when I look back
81. And remember that night
82. I just see him
83. Hollow
84. And
85. He was not a hollow man
86. He was a man that was
87. Full
88. Of life
89. Of spirit
90. Of kindness
91. Of generosity
92. Of anger
93. And
94. Of himself
95. At least that is what I thought
96. Until I look back now
97. Over twenty years later
98. And realize
99. That he was full
100. Only of her

THE CHAMBERS

There are four
Parts
Of me
That I need
So desperately
Each one
Relies
On the other
Just like
A sister or brother
All equal
All separate
All one
They are
My pulse
My spirit
My dreams
My realities
Pasts and futures
Four chambers
Holding love
Undivided
By distance
Or death

A BOY AND HIS DOG

After they left he cried himself to sleep.

It had been a horrible few days. *Why did they have to move here? I told them not to move at all. I hate them.* His mind was fueled by anger and regret. Anger because he had been ignored and regret because he had failed to act. The boy was eleven. His name was Billy.

After an hour of tears he drifted off. He was fully dressed in his blue jeans with turned-up cuffs and a white T-shirt with ketchup stains from dinner.

Billy was dreaming now.

He was alone in a white room. He could hear arguing. Yes versus no. The voices shouted. The shouting got louder and louder, soon turning to shrieks. A wagon wheel flew at him from behind. It just missed his head and shattered like glass in midair. The pieces fell to the ground as rose petals. A collie licked them up and fell ill.

While the boy was dreaming, his mother and father were arriving at their destination with the dog secured and cramped in the backseat of the Thunderbird. "Is this it?" she said. "This looks bad."

"Make like a sphinx," the husband said. "We don't have a choice."

The boy's dog was named Kippy. The boy and his parents, Jim and Norma, had picked out Kippy as a puppy five years ago on a rainy night just like this one. Now Kippy was in trouble just for doing what dogs sometimes do. Kippy looked around and let out a low whimper to signal he was getting uncomfortable. "Relax," she said. "We can get out soon." Her husband parked the car in the driveway but left the engine on. "A smoke," he said. She started to cry, and he knew they had to talk.

The boy bolted up. He knew it was a dream. He turned and put his head back on the pillow. He was tired. So much had happened so fast. He felt like it was all his fault. Over and over he saw the images of the event in his mind. The leash he left behind. The swing set. The metal cart. The track. The girl's scream. The adults running. The blood. The police. The crate. Barking. All bad.

His father and mother explained it like this: "It's really nobody's fault ... but now we face a difficult situation ... you have to try to understand ... he punctured her skin ... it was not a nip ... I know the wheel ran over his foot ... yes, but she got hurt, and if it happened to you ... no, we can't keep him ... please stop crying ... we can visit him for a while, maybe ... he will be okay ... please stop asking that ... we don't have a choice ... the police will check ... this letter they sent is serious ... stop crying, please ... it's nobody's fault ... yes, she will be okay ... I tried, but they didn't listen ... we have no choice."

He drifted back to sleep in the bed he used to share.

The boy's father decided to try to avoid any discussion and go through with the plan. He turned off the engine and started to get out of the car to get the dog.

"What are you doing?" she asked.

"Getting the dog," he said.

"Sit down, please. Do we have to go through with this?" she asked.

"They will sue us," he said. "For a lot of money. The girl had to get shots, for Jesus's sake."

"He loves that dog," she said, "and we love him."

All three of them sat in silence.

They saw the porch light go on in the house at the end of the driveway, and then the door opened and a man and woman and boy came out. Illuminated by a lamppost, the man walked toward the car. "Shit," Billy's father said as he got out of the car to meet the man who was coming to get the dog.

"Howdy," the man said. "That's my wife and son up there, and hot diggity, are they excited to see you. Trouble with the dog? You've been parked here a few minutes; thought there might be a problem with the dog. Where is he? Oh, in the backseat. I can scoot around and get the bugger. This is exciting ...my son is ready for this. Nice car, friend. Roger Tuttle. You are Jim ... Jim Barnes, right?"

The boy's mother could hear all of that and wrapped the leash more firmly around her wrist.

The boy's father was out of the Thunderbird. "Don't touch the door, Tuttle," said the boy's father. "We are keeping the dog. Misunderstanding."

"Hey. What?" said Tuttle. "Mis-*what*? Now that's my boy's dog, friend."

"The dog stays in the car and with us. It was a mistake. Not your fault. Here's two hundred. Buy your boy his own dog."

Jim got back in the car. Norma could see the woman on the porch holding her son closer.

As they drove away, they could hear Tuttle yelling that they were lying bastards.

An hour later they were home. Norma went into the house to pay the babysitter and check on Billy. Jim walked Kippy quickly and she was downstairs when he came in.

"He's asleep," she said. "Dressed. I can tell he was crying."

"Make us a drink?" he asked.

She made each of them a VO, and up they went with Kippy to the boy's room.

Billy was on top of the covers with his head at the foot of the bed.

Kippy quickly moved into the room and up to Billy's face and started licking.

The boy was confused. His dog was home. How? His parents came closer, and his mother sat on the bed and his dad stood next to her. "What happened?" Billy asked.

"We just couldn't do it," she said.

Jim took a sip of his VO and thought of his older brother, Jack, born 1930, now deceased, riding on the back of the family dog, Buppo, in 1938.

A CLUE?

This hand is weaker now
These eyes see less
This voice is softer
Than before
The gait is slower
The pace delayed
Breathing shallow
All senses reduced
Except listening
To the past
Hoping to hear again
A clue
From you

A PRAYER FOR THE PRAYERLESS

When it is unimaginable
We must imagine

When it is unthinkable
We must think

When it is unacceptable
We must accept

When it is incomprehensible
We must comprehend

When it is unbearable
We must bear

When it is hopeless
We must hope

When it is
We must

THE JOURNEY

We see a human emerge.

Out of the wilderness.

From a darker place.

From inside a deep forest.

Cold.

Very little light at the ground level.

Glimpses of sun above.

Rain.

Sometimes chilling wind. Sometimes unknown sounds.

Predators?

The man is now a man alone.

He turns slowly in each direction of the compass he no longer has.

It is broken on the ground next to him.

He broke it in a fit of rage at his predicament.

Alone.

Cold.

No way out.

Frightened.

The man turns repeatedly.

Making small steps in a given direction.

Then stopping.

And turning again.

Lost.

So very lost.

He looks back.

Is that back?

He is disoriented.

At times, paralyzed.

Will he die here?

How did he get to this place?

Memory weak.

Filled with doubt.

Which way to go?

Where are the dangers?

Where is it safe?

Who can tell?

Who can tell the difference?

It is darker now.

The man calls familiar names.

No answers.

Silence.

Silence for so long.

It is very cold.

Wind blows against him.

He must protect himself.

How?

Alone now.

How long has it been?

There are shadows.

In this darkness.

He speaks to the shadows.

To ease the fear.

No response.

Silent shadows in a dark, cold place.

Where is he?

And he goes on and on.

Thoughts swirling.

Changing him.

Worrying him.

So cold his hands go to his pockets.

The paper he feels for what feels like the first time concerns him when he reads:

"You may die."

As he crumples it, he sees writing on the other side.

"You may live."

He puts the paper back in his pocket.

Now it is snowing, and more wind pushes him forward and back.

The snow sticks to the frozen leaves.

Time passes, and he sees footprints ahead of him in the snow.

Who is here?

He follows the tracks.

He walks bent over so he can see more clearly through the increasing darkness.

Who?

Who?

Where?

They are his own, he thinks.

But he is not sure.

Of anything.

He calls out and gets no response.

He stops moving.

He tries not to move at all or breathe or think.

He just waits for something to happen.

What might happen?

He worries.

What's next?

Nothing is next.

That worries him.

He moves off again.

He is hungry now, too.

He makes some noise as he walks.

He stops to listen to the noise.

Nothing.

He does this three times, and every time the noise stops when he stops.

The prints were his?

Then on the fourth time the noise does not stop.

He worries now about the noise.

It gets louder.

The noise is approaching.

The man turns repeatedly to see the source of the noise.

It is close.

So close.

He sees nothing.

He shivers.

The noise stops.

You are lost. You need help. Let me see your note.

The man is terrified. He hears the voice but cannot see anyone.

Look.

Finally the man makes an effort to see through the snow.

And the dark.

And the sadness he feels.

He is exhausted by his attempts.

He finally thinks he sees an outline of a small manlike thing standing directly in front of him.

Give me the note.

His fear pushes his hand to retrieve the note.

As he extends the note to the figure, the snow slowly stops, and he can see it looks like a man.

Short.

In a Marines cap.

Holding a stick with a flashlight taped to the tip.

Like a bayonet?

This short man is wearing a well-worn red wool overcoat and pants but no shoes.

The prints were his own.

If you want, I can help you now.

Yes. I am lost. I need to go back.

Which way is back? Aren't you cold?

Back depends on you.

How far back, and from where, and why do you need me for that?

I warm myself most of the time. It is only cold sometimes. I am not here long.

The barefoot man walks next to the man lost.

Do you know why you are here? Do you know how this happened?

The barefoot man asks questions without waiting for answers.

They journey like this together for a long time, it seems.
But the man is not sure how long.

You have been headed in the right direction, as there is only one direction one can go.

But you have not gone directly.

Follow the path.

I do not see a path.

It is yours to see.

Use your flashlight to lead the way.

Go first.

I will be here while you need me.

Still cold inside and out, the man feels better.

Not as alone.

The man walks ahead first.

He cannot hear footsteps behind him.

So he looks back often to see if he is alone or not.

21

He is not alone until he is.

The last time he looks back, all he sees is the stick with the flashlight taped to the tip.

It is pointed straight up.

The flashlight is on, glowing toward the sky, revealing the renewed intensity of the snow.

The man calls out for the companion.

Nothing.

The man searches for footprints.

Nothing.

He thinks, what do I do now?

I do nothing, he thinks.

He stares at the pointed stick.

What does it mean?

Are there footprints?

None.

Now he is confused.

Colder now.

More snow, and now sleet.

The man approaches the stick left behind.

He will need it to find his way.

To hunt, perhaps.

Or for heat?

It was a gift, he thinks.

But why?

The man pulls the stick from the snowbank.

With two hands, he points it to light his way.

That is when he feels something strange on the stick.

He runs his hands over the strangeness.

The tips of his fingers follow grooves in the wood.

It is so dark.

Too dark to see.

Symbols? Letters?

They feel like letters.

L? Y? d?

The man pulls the flashlight from the tip of the stick and turns it to the grooves.

Learn to make your own light.

The man starts walking again in the same direction.

The stick helps him.

The light helps him.

But he still feels so lost.

He is thirsty and hungry and tired and confused.

Why did he leave me alone?

He walks, maybe straight, maybe not.

He cannot tell.

He thinks of his past but cannot remember much.

The snow tastes good, and that works for a while.

But a while turns into hours and what must be days.

He cannot tell how long is long.

Exhausted, he tries to rest, but it is too cold to stop, yet too harsh to continue.

He remembers things, from a life ... some cold ... some harshness ... now some family ... some jobs ... some ... some ... some losses ... some successes ... some failures ...

His life?

The flashlight is running out as he collapses.

The snow has stopped when the sound of children singing wakes him up.

There is light now.

Day?

Maybe he was not wandering as long as he thought.

Or is he dead?

He does not feel dead, but has never been dead himself.

So many he knows have died, yet he cannot ask them what it feels like to be dead.

But he is an expert in what it feels like not to be alive.

This is not that.

The children's voices sound close.

He forces himself to move through the snow, up a steep hill, with three trees on top.

Up he goes toward the voices.

It is even colder toward the top of the hill.

He tries to move faster and faster.

He uses the stick to push up and up.

The flashlight falls out of his pocket.

At last he stands next to the three trees and looks down the other side of what he has climbed.

His side was steep, but the other side has three descending plateaus.

He sees children playing on the three gentler slopes on their side of the hill.

The children are sledding.

It is as he stands there for a few minutes, staring at the sight, that his feet feel frozen in place.

There are, he counts ... four children.

Yes.

Two boys ... two girls.

And a dog.

Ages unknown.

Maybe seven, eight?

He calls to them.

HELLO?
HELLO THERE.
CAN YOU HELP ME?
I'M LOST. I AM STUCK.

They all turn to him and then sing:

CAN YOU HELP ME?
CAN YOU HELP ME?
WE THINK NOT.
WE THINK NOT.
YOU ARE THE ADULT HERE.

YOU ARE THE ADULT HERE.
YOU HELP US.
YOU HELP US.

When done, they start playing again.

The dog is nipping at the children's heels, which hang off the backs of the sleds.

One boy stands on his sled and takes off down the three plateaus ... and flips over after stopping too fast.

This boy gets up and does it again and again and again.

STOP. YOU'LL GET HURT.

WHERE ARE WE?

The children no longer pay attention to him.

Except one boy. The one in the red wool coat does stop.

From the bottom of the hill, the boy turns to the man.

Come down the hill first. To the middle, then you will see. Come to the middle.

First the singing, now this.

The boy starts walking up the hill.

Meet me halfway.

The man is stuck in the snow. He cannot move down to the boy.

The man manages to free his feet, but he cannot go in the direction the boy is.

He tries.

And tries.

The boy loses interest waiting in the middle for the man and returns to his friends to continue playing.

That is done now.

The man's feet are free, and since he can only go back the way he came, he does.

It somehow feels good to go in that direction.

Yet it is in exactly the opposite direction he was going before.

Proceeding back down the hill he just climbed, he notices a glass house.

It is right there in front of him.

He approaches the house and then stops to take it in.

Glass.

All the walls are glass.

And the roof.

And windows and the picket fence.

Glass.

All glass.

The snow is back. It makes it harder to see.

But there is a glow from inside the glass.

Inside a feast is in progress.

Food, drink, and the noise of a hundred guests.

At first he sees just two women.

He calls to them, but they are not aware of his presence.

He is hungry.

The women in the glass house ignore him.

They are busy taking care of their guests.

Now there are so many half-familiar faces.

Enjoying themselves at times.

But in some rooms, crying.

So frustrating to see in, and not enter.

He watches, occasionally summoning them, in vain.

Time to move on?

Time to move on.

The man turns to leave and walks a few feet from the house to an open mailbox.

A cane lies against the box. A flashlight is in the box, along with an envelope.

In the envelope he finds seven pictures, one for each day of the week.

Monday's is a bowling alley.

Tuesday's shows two men drinking and playing gin.

Wednesday's is a man asleep in his bed wearing an eye patch.

Thursday's he sees two old women folding laundry.

Friday's is a fish.

Saturday's is a child's bare feet on a diving board.

Sunday's is blank.

He thinks about things differently now.

Like he is ...history.

Not old,

Not young,

Not now,

Not then,

But history.

He thinks all he experienced is himself now, pushing forward in a space in which he is very small.

I am history.

Or a small speck of it.

Or, to some, a larger speck?

The snow continues to fall, and he cannot tell the time.

After a while, the snow turns slowly to sleet, then slowly to a rain, then quickly to a dense fog as the temperature increases.

The fog engulfs him now.

He is no longer cold.

He hears something.

A bird?

Birds?

A flock of cardinals, in a single line, flies past, less than a foot above him.

It seemed to him as if they cut a path through the fog.

He pushes on in the direction they went.

The fog becomes his home.

He moves through it almost comfortably,

At home in the peaceful grayness.

After some time, the length of which is unknown to him, he reaches an area of transition.

The cardinals have long disappeared.

And the man stands on a line in the ground with fog at his back.

He observes, for the first time, bright sun and sand in front of him.

He pauses, motionless.

Forward or back?

He steps away from the fog and feels sand below his feet.

A desert is all around him now.

He pauses to look circularly about.

The fog behind him?

Gone.

As far as he can see, sand and sand and sand and ...

It is hot.

Bright sun beats on him.

A new discomfort.

On he goes.

His feet pushing through the hot sand.

The wind in his face.

Straining forward.

Looking.

Looking.

The man uses his memories as energy to proceed.

His thoughts propel him forward.

And sideways.

And once or twice backward, surprising him.

But he presses on through the hot, dry, sandy place he is in.

Thirsty,

So thirsty.

The air turns still.

No wind.

Just sun.

Then ahead ...

A flash.

He moves toward this faraway flash.

He is going to walk a long time.

But in two steps, he is upon the source of the flash.

An oasis is in front of him.

How did it get so close so fast?

He observes what he can.

Four pools of water of varying sizes.

And depths?

He steps closer.

Now each pool is surrounded with palm trees.

And grass.

And two wooden folding chairs.

33

In the middle there is a box.

Inside the man finds many locks and many keys.

He tries all the combinations.

It seems that one key opens all the locks.

The four areas are now about him.

He is in the center,

Turning like his old compass to take it all in.

As he completes his circular review, the third pool begins to dry up.

And its palm tree withers.

The sun is so hot.

And the air is so dry.

What can he do?

He is helpless.

He can do nothing to help.

He shouts for it to stop.

Too late.

It is gone.

The three remaining pools and palm trees protect him now.

And he stays a while to enjoy what he now has.

BEFORE YOU FALL

When the outside gets too cold
You go inside.

It happens to us all.

When the pain gets too hard
You go inside.

Before you fall.

When it hurts your eyes to see
And it hurts your ears to hear
And it hurts your heart to beat,
You go deep inside.

To another place
You make up.

So you can live
Without the pain
Without the cold.

To a place
To warm your heart
For a while by a
Fire that isn't there
But needs to be.

It happens to us all,
Or else
We fall.

A EULOGY

BEFORE YOU FALL

All he could hear on the way up to the podium was the clicking sound of his heels against the cold marble floor of the church. Loud, cold clicks that he associated with the heartbeat of the man he was and the father he was to eulogize.

The phone rang Sunday afternoon, December 5th, and when he answered it he heard his brother tell him that their father had expired and that someone had to go to the hospital to make arrangements for the body to be removed and sent to a funeral home. His family was at the kitchen table, but he did not remember talking to them, not even talking to his soon-to-be ex-wife who would react very poorly to the demise of the patriarchal figure in her life. He slowly went out the backdoor and got into his car, the same car he would catch his wife riding in with her tennis instructor/lover, and drove to the hospital.

He was familiar with the route. He estimated that he had made this 1.1 mile trip at least 250 times over the past four years. First to visit his father. Then his mother. Then his father again. With a few uncounted trips to see his aging grandmother before she checked in to the Sunny Way Nursing Home in order to recuperate from the stroke, it was easily over two-fifty.

He pulled into the same hospital parking lot that he had pulled into eighteen years before to be present at the birth of his first daughter. He walked in the backdoor of the hospital as if he were an employee returning to work. He knew the way to his father's deathbed like the back of his hand. Up the elevator, to the right, around the nurses station on the left, three doors past the smell of urine, and forty years into the past.

No problem until he got to the door of his dead dad's room. It was a double room. The heads of the beds were against the left-side wall. The bed closest to the door was empty, with the sheets removed, exposing an unused mattress. The curtain was pulled back, and on the bed table he could see a bedpan and water pitcher. The buzzer hung lifeless over the edge of the bedrail. The curtain of the far bed, which had been home for his father for the last several weeks was pulled, shutting out his view of the body. He glanced around the hall but did not see anyone he could stall with, so he stared at the curtain and tried to look through it, to see slowly what he knew he would see all at once.

He moved into the room up to the curtain, and as his angle changed he saw toes and the bottom of his father's legs through a space between the curtain and the wall. Soon he could take in his father's entire dead body.

He was nude on the bed, his eyes and mouth wide open, and he seemed to be gasping for air. But he was still. It was more an outline, really. Like a pencil sketch of a landscape curved across the horizon, distant rolling hills past an open mouth in a head tilted back ever so slightly so that his chin appeared like a bluff over the range of his chest, gray with tumbleweed, resting near the boney crevices of his legs, which pointed straight down to toenails that stood sharp and ragged, splintered from the elements.

He would find himself compelled to sketch this view as a single line on a white sheet of paper or on a napkin at a bar or in a meeting or in the sand while at the beach with his children on a happy summer day.

The voice from the podium began, and it sounded strong and sincere. Like it was supposed to. A loving, thankful voice. Firm with manliness. Anger loyally repressed:

My father was like many men, a complicated man like many men, he was a strong family man like many men, who loved his wife and children ...

Like many men ...

Which is why my brothers and I are here ...

Like many men today ...

In remembrance of our father ...

Like many fathers ...

He looked through the casket in front of the altar and X-rayed the outlined relief of the body inside and wondered about the inner landscape of the man before him. Who was it in there? How had this man felt when he was alone? What were his memories of the life they shared, and how could he have been such an enigma? What did he remember?

Did he remember the last time they spoke?

It was in the hospital, about a week ago, the culmination of five years of sickness, weakness, and transfusions brought on by a form of leukemia contracted, they believed, as a result of entering Nagasaki as a Second Division Marine, forty-five days after the bomb was dropped.

His father's lungs were filling up with his own white blood cells, erroneously fighting an infection that was not there. In a sense, through a misunderstanding, he killed himself. Very true, only he had started killing himself forty years earlier.

His father was still and very thin. This huge man of his youth was fragile and frightened. His father's blue eyes called to his son. Shot right through him.

Tell me, they said. *Tell me, do something, help me, you must help me.*

The son could do nothing for him. He just denied what he needed to, waiting for his father to get up from bed, clear his throat, and walk to the window to smoke a cigarette and pull out a single to play liar's poker. This did not happen.

His father only kept looking up. Longing. Waiting for one of his three sons to say or do something, to fix things.

No one did anything, yet.

The eldest son looked directly down into his father's sick blue eyes. He could reach out to touch him but instead held the bedrail. Their eyes were less than two feet apart, but it felt like fifty years. The father was sixty-three; the son was thirty-seven, but a part of him felt as if he were still nine. Nine years old. He was nine when he learned, taught himself really, to hate his father, to fear him, to reject him for most of what he was and to stop admitting he loved him for all he was and was not. Nine, when he buried that part of himself that loved and needed him. Worshipped him.

The thirty-seven-year-old son stood inches away from his sixty-three-year-old father and was lost in the confusion of a distant nine-year-olds perception of an out-of-control, alcoholic, promiscuous, angry, tormented and loving dad. It was, the son would learn later, just a misunderstanding.

The father was sixty-three and dying. The son was still nine. It was December. Cold outside. The hospital room was warm. His father had no shirt on. His neck was long between his head and body. It strained like a chicken's. In the hall, the doctors had explained all the limited options.

He had a day or two at most. They could operate and put a hose into the older man's lungs and force in medicine that might or might not work. That might or might not add a day or two of life, and pain.

The brothers voted, looking to the eldest for the right vote to cast. They would do nothing. They would let their father die.

Back in the room, the father searched and found his thirty-seven-year-old son's eyes. "Where do we go from here?" he asked in what was left of his marine corporal's voice. The son was silent, but inside, without hesitation, he screamed, *straight to hell*.

He saw his own children in the pews listening to him, or not, as he spoke loudly in glorious intonations about their grandfather and his accomplishments, and knew at that moment that he was exactly the same as the man he loved and despised and that he was a corrupted version of a corrupted version of a man and a father and a husband ... but he chose to ignore that fact and proceeded with the half-lie that was his eulogy and that was, by then, already the fabric of his own life.

He knew the funeral service was to end two hours later at a cemetery on a hill where the body of his father was to be placed in a crypt next to his mother's home in the wall of bodies.

His mother had been the wife, for forty years, of today's dead man. The man who loved her beyond his own capacity to understand that love. The man who tortured her with betrayals and adorned her with gifts. The powerful man with the undiagnosed broken heart she had unwillingly left behind just six months ago.

The eulogist rarely visited his mother's crypt. She was the loving but perpetual child of Mary (ensconced in a nursing home and to die in three months) and William Sr. (deceased following a life of postal service and despair), tolerating sister of William Jr. (deceased age fifty, leaving behind two devoted daughters and a loving wife), grateful and awed niece of Katherine (ensconced in a nursing home and to die in four months), emotionally distant yet remarkably present mother of the eulogist and his brothers, and indulgent grandmother of three grandchildren already born and a fourth she would never meet.

His father struggled until the end. He struggled to survive death. He struggled to survive life. He was a Marine, a tough guy; he was the firstborn older brother, who never cried.

He was just another man among millions of men.

But the only one who mattered.

He was sunshine and darkness. Good and evil. A man who needed to be loved and did not know it or show it. He was a father to a son. A hero and an enemy. A nightmare in a suit.

He was the man the son tried to be so different from, and the man the son needed so much to be like.

Surveying the church, the son, finishing out loud, said:

...The one we all admired and emulated ...

...The limousines are waiting now to take us to the cemetery ...

...Thank you for sharing this day with us.

A WOMAN PICKING BERRIES

A woman picking berries
One by one
Like the days of her life
Each one put into a basket
With the others
And taken away
She sees it that way
Picking one after the other
Individually
Like the steps she took
Away from love
One after the other
So many collected
In such a short time
So many not collected
She sees it that way
The woman picking berries
All day
Every day
Having to choose
Which one to pick
So that others would
Be happy
From her picking
So many berries
She is sixty now
So many berries picked
She can't remember
Her first
It was just for a few days
Until she could save

Some money
To save herself
The berries kept coming
No matter how fast she picked
Her days flew by
In bushels
Her children too
While she picked
They grew
She sees it that way
Now she does
But not then
Berry after berry
Hands trained to
Pick
And let go
She sees it that way

ALL THE DAYS

Another day
Passes
Any day
And
You are sixty-two
Many days
Behind you
Filled ones
Empty ones
Happy hearts
Broken hearts
Days and nights
Too long
Too short
All the days
Remembered
Or
Forgotten
Days and days
Then
Another
Birthdays
Deathdays
You add them up
Subtract them down
I am here
Now
I was there
Then
And tomorrow?

43

BOILING THE BINKIES

It was an emergency of sorts. His son's binkies were on the counter next to the stove when he dropped the sugar bowl and it shattered into small porcelain pieces. So he had to open the new ones, and the instructions required him to boil them for five minutes before first use.

But first he had to clean the stovetop and kitchen floor where the sugar bowl bomb went off. Then make dinner. Then help with the dishes. Then play with his wife and son. Then help clean up. Then boil the binkies before his wife finished getting their son ready for bed.

Finally, as mom and son went upstairs, in they went.

He noticed that binkies float, so at any given time only half a binky was boiling. He upped the required time to about ten minutes and started stirring. Around they went. Occasionally, he held them underwater with his spoon, but for the most part he watched them boil and just stirred.

The binkies seemed to enjoy the boiling water, splashing and jumping around in their little bathtub. Just like his children used to do.

He was a grandfather now. His oldest child was thirty-five. His youngest was only eighteen months. But they all shared the innocent joy of a baby's bathtub. The squeals. The suds. The smiles.

The binkies swirled, and he saw the faces of his dead parents. Peaceful, swirling faces he lost over twenty years ago. He tried to imagine his grandparents giving a bath to his parents when they were still young enough to squeal. He remembered a small, faded picture of his great-aunt, sitting in a porcelain bowl at about age two. The image was faded, but he knew there was a smile on the little girl's face.

He thought, *The faded water was not boiling. The faded porcelain was not broken.* But that was a long time ago. His great-aunt had died the same year his parents did. So did one grandfather. And one grandmother. And his mother's brother.

He had stirred the binkies now for over twenty years, but still had nine minutes to go.

CHISELING

A forceful blow
Or
A delicate tweak
Designed to break
Or shape
An object
To split it
Or shorten it
Or curve it
Distorting it
For better or worse
From the original
Usually performed
Quickly
And
Repeatedly
With no regard
For the opinion
Of
The object

COLLECTING STRING

He is older
Now
Resting
By the window
Looking out
At the daytime
The world rushing by
On empty sidewalks
He looks out
From the old couch
Collecting string
In little balls
Or bigger ones
Or rubber bands
Or memories
Time spent
Wasted
Or time
Invested well
Slowly
He works
And slowly
The stings unwind
The rubber hardens
And
The memories change too

THE SUN

The sun appears
Up every
Morning
Stays for the
Required time
Sharing light
For the time
Permitted
Then seems
To set
Casting us
Into darkness
The sun
Just shines
Singular
Watching us
In motion
We initiate
The darkness
The sun
Waits
Motionless
For our return

SAM'S

THE SUN

Jim had about an hour left before he had to meet his wife at his son's school for a concert. As he left the mall, after returning some clothes, he decided to stop to grab some lunch. He knew a rather large deli located in a small shopping strip right off the highway. His wife had reminded him this morning how important today was. Their son wanted both of them to see him perform. Jim would be in and out of the deli in less than fifteen minutes.

He pulled in and quickly found a parking space. It had started to rain lightly, but he didn't mind. Once inside, he ordered a chicken cutlet on whole wheat and took a no-pulp orange juice from the cold case. Maybe he should have had the salmon, he thought. Or the pasta. He paid and headed out.

He remembered there was a drugstore three doors away, so he went there for some hand wipes and Q-Tips. He walked leisurely in the rain to the drugstore and began thinking about the supermarket that used to be where the drugstore was. It was a Bohack's back then.

Then.

Then was 1957.

He would have been about nine. Now he was sixty.

He found the wipes in aisle six and the Q-Tips in aisle eleven. He paid for both while considering asking the clerk if she knew what her drugstore used to be. She was about twenty-one.

He didn't ask.

He left into the rain again and stopped briefly for a moment outside the exit. His car was parked to his left, but he turned right and walked slowly to the corner of the shopping strip. He could see the Mobil gas station still on the corner after all these years. His first job had been pumping gas there when he was fifteen. The old liquor store was now a shoe store.

He stopped at the entrance to the first store on the strip. Now it sold highly fashionable clothes for highly fashionable young women.

48

There were double glass doors that revealed the interior, and Jim opened the door on the right and stepped in onto the raw concrete floor and under the bright white lights. The store was full of racks of hot new items that his youngest daughter might be too old for.

An attractive young sales girl asked if he needed any help. *Yes*, he thought, *but not about clothes*.

"No," he said. "Just looking."

And he was looking.

First at the concrete floor, then at the blouse-covered walls. Then he assessed the depth and width of the interior of this store. Slowly? Or was it in an instant? The old Sam's Candy and Cigar Store that occupied this space in 1957 reappeared in every detail.

They would burst through the creaky door on the right after jumping off their bikes after riding for twenty minutes from home, down busy and not-so-busy streets, as fast as possible, skidding when they could, pedaling as hard as they could with strong, young legs and having as much fun as they could with free, open hearts.

Everything then was about what they could do. They were eight to ten years old. Unstoppable, alive, and vibrant. He remembered all of them. Webster Hurley. David Gershwin. Stephen (Little Steve) Pollack. Ellen Pollack. Scott Bazaar. And Big Steve (who never had a last name).

Into Sam's they would go.

Into the dimly lit store that sold cigars, newspapers, magazines, comics, school supplies, toys, trinkets, socks, and counter food— including brown hamburgers, bacon and eggs all day, sandwiches if you liked rye, and ice-cold milkshakes that always had a dividend left in the silver mixer that didn't fit into your tall glass on the first pour.

It was well worth the quarter.

He felt he could smell Sam's now. The mix of the still air and all they sold blended with the presence and odor of the two brothers who owned Sam's and were the sole employees. *They* were Sam and his brother, who they all called "the other Sam."

Jim saw the brothers behind the cash register area at the front of the store. "Hello, Jimmy," Sam would always say. "New comics in the back." Sam was a short man who was barely visible behind the counter. Sometimes the children would have to push the money toward the register so Sam could reach it. The other Sam said nothing for the whole five years Jim remembered going there. The other Sam was always busy doing something important. Unpacking boxes. Arranging magazines. Wiping the counter. Cooking. Always with that cigar, and whiskers. Just enough to look hung-over, which reminded Jim of his father on a Sunday morning. Or almost any morning.

The transformation was almost complete.

He was swept up in it now. Without moving, his feet firmly on the concrete floor where once the linoleum rested, Jimmy roamed the old haunt. Over to the magazine rack. Around the displays of art supplies, down the toy aisle, emerging at the seven-stool lunch counter. As usual, he found an empty seat and climbed up and poked his head around for the other Sam. Jimmy was hungry now. The other Sam appeared, and Jimmy ordered a chocolate milkshake. The other Sam turned to make it, and Jimmy ran to get a comic and take a quick peek at the *Playboys* on the top rack.

Miss September stared down at Jimmy. She reminded him of someone he would meet ten years from now. He would meet her in high school. Marry her after college. She would leave him for their children's tennis instructor twelve years into the marriage and six months after his parents would die.

Jimmy shook that off and grabbed the new Superman comic. The cover showed Superman experiencing kryptonite for the first time. Jimmy understood vulnerability. Superman was lucky. Adults were far more plentiful than kryptonite.

The milkshake was ready when Jimmy returned with the comic. Before he could finish pouring most of the shake into his glass, he heard the front door and Sam say "Hi, Webby. New comics in the back." It was ten-year-old Webster Hurley. Jimmy liked Webster. He was from Chicago and had moved next door to Jimmy a year ago. They had a love of comics and dinosaurs in common. Webster was skinny, wide-eyed, and very athletic. Everyone called him Webby, which Webster liked. Webby and Jimmy would pretend to be dinosaurs by squatting and pulling their shirts tightly over their knees and trying to knock each other over. Powerful friends with powerful imaginations.

Jim knew that Webby would move back to Chicago in another year. Jim also knew he would look his best friend up thirty years after that and discover a high school memorial page in Webster's honor.

Jimmy shared his milkshake with Webby so they could pool their money and buy comics.

Soon Webby wanted to leave, but Jimmy didn't want to leave. Not Sam's. Not Webby. Not then. Webster grabbed the comics and put his share of the money down in a spot where he knew Sam would have to really try hard to get it. "Let's go," he said, as he bolted out the door to his bike.

Jimmy just stared at the doors. A woman entered, and the spell was broken. Jim put his share of the change back in his pocket. It was time. He had his son's concert to go to. "Excuse me," said a sales girl. "May I help you?"

"No thanks," said Jim as he looked past her, through her really, trying to find Sam's. As Jim slowly walked out the door, he thought about looking back but didn't. He just headed for his parked car.

Less than five minutes had passed. It surprised him that still had plenty of time. As he drove the four miles to his son's school, he relived what he had just relived - over and over, in detail, trying to understand what had happened. It is true that he was sad about Webster's death, but no sadder than the deaths of his parents, grandparents, cousins aunts, uncles, godparents, and some adult friends, all of whom were gone too soon.

In a larger sense, it was true that he missed the past, but not as much as he loved the present. Sure, the present wasn't perfect. Neither was the past. Neither was his second marriage. But each marriage blessed him with children whom he would never trade for the past.

The driver of the car behind Jim's leaned on the horn so long and loud it finally brought Jim out of his inertia.

Jim gunned the gas pedal, and on he went. And on he thought.

Over and over he ran through the memories of those minutes/days in Sam's. His cell phone rang, and it was his oncologist's office confirming his appointment for blood work and a CT scan the next morning. "Sure," he said. "Be there 9:30 a.m." He had it on his calendar since the last one.

And his wife had reminded him this morning before she left with their son for school. How could he forget stage three colon cancer?

Jim knew that the cancer was weakening his body. Now he saw it as his mental kryptonite, destroying his superpowers of self-esteem and confidence. He felt safe in Sam's. So he was looking for a safe place? How could that help? Confused, Jim turned up the radio and made a right onto the long, winding driveway of his son's school.

There were just a few parking spaces at the back of the school parking lot. But he wasn't late.

He had promised his son he would be there for him.

And he had to make sure he made it.

HIS LAST BEDTIME STORY

stare at ceiling
can't
eyes shut against will
dying
stroke
paralyzed
incommunicado
can hear
can think
can't move
can remember
memory good
too good
tastes
smells
moments
fifty
years ago
yesterday
bullets
Saipan
car crash
broken nose
sex
seventeen
Mary dead
last breath
my stroke
sixty-two
cancer
hurts to remember

can't not
lost her
my fault
too soon
too young
me too
why
what happened
strong
weaker
dead
fast
alone
stroke
regret
fights
confused
sons helping
lost
lost
afraid
bills
business
Mary
gone
all gone
all
not me
not Jim
still owes me
she knew
right again
gone
money gone
dad gone
mom gone
sweet Jesus

Mary gone
oh god gone
I remain
remains
my remains
no money
bills
house
pain
life over
fast
fast
fast
three boys
cheating
drinking
fights
love
love
fast
love
broken heart
golf
love golf
love Mary
love kids
afraid
alone
so alone
Brooklyn
young then
fresh
now
voices laugh
no pain
food
beer

priests
cards
pool
late nights
hot
bowling
Mary
high school
god
so pretty
smooth
smell
touch
family
okay
okay
boys
all men
me gone
Mary gone
family
can't help
help me
help
help help help
no use
no words
pictures
swimming
remember
water
sun
sand
kids
beach
Mary
gin

sex
fun
no fight
no fight
then
not always
loud
good point
always right
bad
sorry
Mary dead
how
so fast
she knew
she knew
stupid
doctors stupid
me stupid
all stupid
she knew
she cared
past now
gone
look ahead
to what
to what
dead soon too
kids okay
business ruined
so what
time wasted
time
so much time
gone
past
spent

drinking
working
money good
life good
regrets
why
can't undo
no point
work mattered
position
everything position
house
family
money
now gone
on my back
no future
I'm out
after her
better
worse
don't know
can't tell
drink
thirsty
not food
sick
gin
ha
gin alone
figures
can't
can't
can't move
can't drink
can't anything
did everything

big deal
now
no matter
no Mary
can't fix
she fixed
always fixed
always watched
good
gentle
nice
too nice
teenager
helped me
shy
no cash
she laughed
rich aunt
limo
she laughed
gave money
helped
a kid
young
free
not dead
not stuck
young
did good
played hard
very
back turned
heart cold
fist hard
Mary
Mary
Mary

waiting
come back
can't
gone now
gone then
love then
gone
gone
lost her
when
babies
work
gin
girls
when
never
maybe
waited
too long
till end
gone now
empty
thirsty
stiff.

PRETEND.

Pretend
I am a Christmas tree,
Grown wild,
Cut for joy
To hold hope
In every light you see.

I stand tall for you,
Branching out,
Awaiting your touch
Filling me out
With glistening decoration,
Straight and wide,
Ready to receive and guard
Your most precious gifts.

Light me up,
Smell me,
Let me make you happy.
Let me entertain you.
Let me fill your heart
With joy
Always.

Wish on me,
Show me off.
Fall asleep beneath my branches.

Pretend
I am all the Christmas trees
You ever had
All together as one.
All your joys
And decorations
And first looks
And presents.

Pretend
I never grow old,
My bulbs never dim,
My branches never dry.

Remember
And enjoy my being
Available to you any day,
Any time
You need a Christmas.

THE BOATING LESSON

The boy really wanted that boat.

The brown hulled plastic one with the three white plastic sails.

The one on the top shelf.

There was only one like it.

"No," she said. "It's too much money."
"No," she said. "You don't need it."
"No," she said. "We can't."
"No."

The boy half knew she was right.

But he wanted the boat.

He now loved the boat that was out of his reach.

It started out quietly, but the boy's insistence quickly grew louder and more piercing.

Within two minutes, the full and well-practiced tantrum was released.

That effort worked to open the purse, and that worked to bring the boat off the top shelf.

She paid for the boat.

The boy was riveted on the clerk's hands as they carefully slipped the boat into a big-enough shopping bag.

The boy failed to notice his mother's face and the tear as she closed her purse and headed to the store exit.

The boy's hands now hugged the boat in the bag.

But there was still so much out of his reach.

She was already in the car when the boy got there.

"Get in carefully," she said.

He did, careful to steady the boat bag on his lap in the front seat.

"Close the door," she said.

He did.

"Watch your fingers," she said.

She did not hear him say okay.

She was thinking about the boat.

It reminded her of what had floated away in her marriage.

The love, and the money too.

What was left?

Now the boy looked at his mother.

Her face looked different to him.

"Are we leaving?" the boy asked.

"We are."

First she lit a Lucky Strike.

Then she started the car and quickly shifted into reverse.

The car shot back out of the parking space, and the boat in the bag and the boy flew forward.

Her right arm shot out to stop him, but her right foot just pressed down harder, and rear of the car quickly hit a telephone pole.

Her neck whiplashed as she saw the plastic boat in the bag come between the boy's head and the dashboard.

She put the car in drive and left the scene as the boy checked to see if the boat was hurt.

GOING UP?

We are shopping.

He is holding my hand, as we go up the escalator, when my nine-year-old son asks:

"Would you save Mom with your life? I mean, die for her? Really, would you?"

No pause, and: "Sure," I say. (*If I don't kill her first*, I think.)

"I thought so," he says, squeezing my hand.

And, we shop for Christmas presents to be placed under a tree where I won't be.

THE PUZZLE

Pieces so small
Only experts would try
Scattered about
Some buried for years
Some with burnt edges
Some torn in half
Any missing?
Carefully touch each one
Feel for a match
It's dark
Try again
Try
For thirty-nine years
Try.
Stop. Try.
Force some pieces
Then start over
Again
And sometimes again
And sometimes not
For sixty-one years
Trying.
So trying
Trying
To put the fragments
Of an original image
Back in place.

THE DRAWER

The couple we see in front of us is fighting.

Again.

Softly at first.

Cutting statements almost whispered.

"You lied." … "You could have done better." … "You …", "You …",
"You …"

Within minutes, the voices escalate and hammer-like insults replace
the undercutting:

"You are so …weak."

"You are pathetic."

This happened almost every time they finished having sex.

But the knock on the door was new.

It startled the arguing pair.

It was 11:00 p.m.

The blonde woman went to her door and asked who it was.

No answer.

The man in his underwear went to the door and asked.

A louder knock.

The man in his underwear squinted through the peephole.

"Shit."

"What?" the blonde woman asked.

"Shit, shit, shit," said the man in his underwear as he stepped back
from the door, looking for his pants.

Even louder pounding on the door, and then from the hall:

"I have the baby."

The blonde woman watched the man in his underwear rifle for his pants
under the covers of the bed in the corner of her studio apartment.

The blonde woman lit a cigarette and peeped through the peephole.

She saw a brunette woman holding a child, and the brunette woman
smacked the peephole.

"Shit."

From the hallway:

"I have the baby, and I am leaving him here."

The man had one leg in his pants as the blonde woman opened the door and said to the face of the brunette,

"You go home with the baby, and *you*" (to the man in half his pants) "you call me when you straighten this out."

The mother, holding the baby like a football, led with her shoulder right into the apartment.

"Where should I put him?"

"Jesus, what are you doing?" the husband said.

"Me?"

Then louder and sadder:

"Where do I put him? Screw you. Screw her. WHERE?"

No one did anything for a few seconds.

Then the baby started to cry.

The mother looked around the studio apartment.

The father struggled to put his left leg in his pants.

The blonde woman went to the kitchenette and made a scotch on the rocks.

"Do you want one, Steve?"

The man finished with his pants and was looking for the rest of his clothes as he grabbed his wallet off the dresser by the only window in the small space that contained all four of them.

The baby was still crying as the brunette went to the dresser and opened the bottom drawer.

The mother pulled out lingerie and underwear and replaced the blonde woman's belongings with her own.

"Oh, God."

The mother's voice was wounded.

"Oh, dear God. You get them both."

As she left, the brunette slapped the blonde and pointed to the baby and said:

"Don't hurt him."

The shocked man, his unbuttoned shirt on by now, was looking back and forth from his son in the drawer to the slapped blonde sipping her scotch, when he heard the blonde ask:

"Now do you want one?"

TOMORROWS

I see so many
Tomorrows
In the faces
Of children
Memories waiting
To hatch
Etchings in progress
Before me
Creating a future
Of wonder
And beauty
Sadness
And regret?
Things to remember
Things to forget
I see so many
Happy faces
Drinking in
The moments
Thirsty for
Everything

I stare
Youthfully
Part of me in now
Part of me in then
Most of me in between
Visiting memories
Of my own
Tomorrows

REGRETS

I am sorry
I have regrets
Regrets
I never wanted
They are
Part of me
Now
Adding weight
To my step

I am sorry
I have regrets
Self-inflicted
Pebbles in my shoes
Reminders
Now
Of pain caused
Loved ones
Liked ones
Living ones
Dead ones
Most ones

I am sorry
I have regrets
Things done
Things said
Things undone
Things not said

71

I am sorry
I have regrets
Now
Charred and frozen
Bits and pieces
Dotting decades

I am sorry
I have regrets
Hanging
Like medals
Of dishonor
On
A well-intentioned
Soul

I am sorry
I have regrets

I regret
I have regrets

Now
I am sorry
They have me.

WHAT I HEAR:

I heard us
From a distance
We must have
Been shouting
Otherwise
How would I
Have heard us
We sounded
Loud
We sounded
Angry
We sounded
Older
Than when
We were
Together
Maybe
We were
Shouting
So we could
Be together
And not
So far
Apart
Maybe
We were
Just loud
Not angry
Maybe
I just heard
The distance

THE FRECKLE

The boy is on the hill in his backyard.
Alone.
A nice day.
He is eight.
He looks at his left hand.
He sees the freckle in the middle of the back of his hand.
I will remember this moment.
I will have this freckle forever.
Staring at his hand, he concentrates as hard as an eight-year-old can.
He would remember what it felt like to be eight.
He would never forget.
But he forgot.
By sixteen he had forgotten his promise to himself.
By twenty-one it was all a blur.
He stares now at his left hand, searching for his youth.
He cannot find the freckle.
All he sees now is the intravenous needle.
One inch above where he thinks the freckle might have been.
He tries to understand all that has happened.
Too much has happened to take in at once.
Too much has happened to take in slowly.
But he does understand.
He understands it all.
He has finally taken it all in.
The good and the bad.
The successes and failures.
The births and deaths.
Starts and stops.
Loves and losses.
Repentance and regret.
He is on the hill.

Remembering the promise he made.
To remember what it felt like to be eight.
No matter how old he got.
Alive.
Full of anticipation.
Unafraid.
The opposite of now.
He smiles to himself.

TODAY

Brick by brick
Grain by grain
We build the fabric of our lives.

Down they go
Piece by stony piece,
The pavement of our existence.

The route we take
Day to day
Moment to moment
Is put in place
By each of us.
Straight,
Narrow,
Wide,
Curved.

Piece by tiny firm piece,
We build
Our paths,
The environment in which we flourish,
Or die,
(Or both).
Step by step
(Planned or random)
We make our way,
Going on from what came before,
Pulling - pushing.

Setting forth our own structures,
Matching the terrain with
Our perceptions of it
So that we become the terrain;
We become the environment.

Piece by piece,
Stone by stone,
Choice by choice,
Up and down they go,
The road and walls of our life,
A life that transports us
At various speeds
And directions
And altitudes
To a final destination.

Or perhaps preventing us
From making a full journey
And
Keeping us traveling
In circles.

Piece by piece, on we go,
Building without a blueprint,
Putting down stones
On a shifting surface.

Putting up walls speck by speck,
That slowly block the light
Until we get used to the dark.
And on we go.
On we go.
We go on.
Each of us with our own

Specks,
Our own perceptions of our terrain,
Perceiving what we must,
Justifying
Why what is done is right.

Piece by piece.
Tick by tick.
Thought by thought.
Creating the world
As it is for us
Today.

LOSS

Alone
I just scream
Sometimes
I don't
Or
I moan
Sometimes
Doing the dishes
Or not
I never know
What sound
I will make
Or when
Sometimes
I remember
The horror
Sometimes
The sound is silent
And hurts
The loudest
Sometimes
The sound
Sounds like
I am broken
And
I am.

MY CARDINAL

A blur at first
Then crimson clarity
Speeding by
Unrestricted
No boundaries
Invisible mostly
But appearing briefly
Don't worry
I am watching
A beacon of observation
In a permanent overcoat
Red and thick
All year long
Stop look at me
How could I not
The red figure
High on the hill
I knew at six
Watching
Still appears
In front of me
A blur at first
Shaping itself slowly
Smiling cold apart thick
Observing all below him
Unrestricted
Appearing briefly

Upon return
Disappearing slowly
Into the VO glass
Before the TV
Don't worry
I am watching
How could I not ...

SINCE THEN

This is
How it is
Since then ...
It's bad
Very bad ...
They all say
It will take a long time
They all say
Very long
We are sorry
They all say
Very sorry
Every word
Every feeling
Every thought
Falls now
Into the abyss
The hollow
Created by absence
The hollow
Expanding daily
To hold the loss
The tears
The fears
The smiles
The miles
Of full years past
And empty years
Yet to be
Awake I hear
The echo

Of the hollow
Asleep
I see inside
The echo
I look for something
In the hollow
To hold onto
Nothing is there
An incalculable void
Insatiably swallowing
Grief
Confusion
Anger
Torment
Hope
Always wanting more
And there is more
Always more
So much more
Slips into the hollow
The hollow prevails
Accepting
What cannot be accepted
Believing
What cannot be believed
Imagining
What cannot be imagined
Holding
What cannot be held
Since then
This is
How it is
I am the hollow.

STILL TWISTING

A tale separated by twenty-eight years

1960—The band was loudly playing rock and roll.
1988—She sat up without her wig.
Everyone was there.
She appeared to be in pain.
It was just 8:00 p.m., and they were finished with dinner.
The bedroom shades were drawn as usual.
The dance floor was getting crowded.
They stared at each other in silence.
He wanted to dance.
She motioned for some water.
He saw her sitting at the table.
He got her a glass of water from the bathroom.
She was talking to her friends.
He helped her drink a little water and sat on the bed.
He walked to her and was pushed and shoved from all sides by the dancers.
She was sixty-two.
When he got to her table, they were playing the Twist.
In a whisper, she asked how he was feeling.
Someone said, "Why don't you dance with your mom?"
Fine, but he could not continue.
"Should we do the Twist?" she asked.
They sat in silence for another five minutes.
Out they went to twist up a storm.
Finally he said, "Can I get you some water?"
They started right in twisting and kept on going for over twenty minutes.
They were alone and could not communicate.
They became the center of attention.

Her eyes closed and her head fell back asleep on the pillow.
"Come on baaay-be, let's do the Twist."
He stared at his mother.
"Take me by the little hand ... and go like this."
She was dying of lung and brain cancer.
He was twisting so hard his side hurt.
She still had beautiful eyes, but the treatments had distorted her face.
By now a circle had formed around them as they out-twisted the crowd.
Only days before, she could still walk slowly around the house and make little jokes.
Up and down and around and around they twisted and twisted.
"Mom ..." *he whispered and touched her swollen hand.*
"Eee-yeah, twist, ba-baaay-by twist ... ooh yeah ... just like this."
It was cold, and he got up without kissing her goodbye.
The music finally stopped; exhilarated and exhausted, they hugged and sat down to applause.
She died that night.
"Not bad for a nine-year-old," she said.

SUBJECT: TOO LONG AGO

Too long ago
The days gone by
Too long ago
The thoughts of why

Too long ago
So many here
Too long ago
No fear of fear

Too long ago
Hands held tight
Too long ago
Now out of sight

Too long ago
The miles ahead
Too long ago
Things left unsaid

Too long ago
Forks in the road
Too long ago
Choices unfold

Too long ago
A future waits
Too long ago
Life hesitates

Too long ago
No regrets to regret
Too long ago
Not yet, not yet

MY LIST

My list of losses
Needs no paperweight
As it rests
For the moment
In a corner
Of my heart
Opposite the list
Of memories,
Next to the list
Of dreams come true,
Under the list
Of I forgot
Each list taking its rightful place,
Filling my heart
With joy
Or sorrow
Or both

SONGS NEVER SUNG

The following is a transcript of audio from a KSL-TV air check dated October 4, 1981, 6:50 p.m. Mountain Time.

Announcer: And now a comment from Mr. William Burke, Station Manager, KSL-TV, Salt Lake City/Provo, Utah.

William Burke: This is Billy Burke, Station Manager KSL-TV.

The news of the plane crash was not big news. Small plane. Local inhabitants. Nobody famous. Not yet, at least. Not yet.

Three people perished on an approach here September 20th, during a rapid snow squall en route from a nightclub appearance in Las Vegas, Nevada. The pilot, Jack Jay, was seriously injured but is expected to recover. The three passengers, all under thirty years old, and all members of a small, mostly unknown but emerging band, perished.

Those who did know them, knew them as The Renegades. Good songs, good folks, who were "on their way to the top," as *The Daily Herald* reported after a local concert at the Symphony Hall in May of 1981. We bid farewell to Norm Walsh, guitar, Jimmy Dix, drums, and the lead singer, Patrick D. B. Bierne.

The Renegades.

It took several days to reach and retrieve the Beechcraft wreckage on King's Peak. The loss of The Renegades probably will not have the same impact as the tragedies of Buddy Holly, Patsy Kline, or other more widely known individuals we have lost, yet this loss was a tragedy nonetheless.

I was a fan. I had seen The Renegades play numerous times. Never met them—my loss. But I loved the band, the music, the renegade spirit.

I came across a letter to the editor yesterday in *The Daily Herald*. Let me read it to you line by line.

LETTERS TO THE EDITOR
THE DAILY HERALD
PROVO, UTAH
October 3rd, 1981

Dear Sirs:

The late Patrick D.B. Bierne was my son.

As you know, he was a great singer-songwriter. His death and the deaths of his friends and fellow band members, Norm Walsh and Jimmy Dix, represented a huge loss to the music world at large and an overwhelming one to me in particular.

We all learned so much from Patrick in his short time here. Especially me.

He was creative and unafraid ... unlike most people I met in my life. All he wanted to do was write and sing, so that in his own way, he could help people.

He adored his brother and sisters as well as his nieces and nephews. He would write short sing-along songs for them when they were young. It occurs to me that he was a great deal like his grandfather, J. Bierne Sr. who was always scribbling something.

I feel Patrick was just hitting his stride as an artist. His most famous, albeit, local hit was "An Empty Heart." He recorded a single of it in 1980. I hope D.J.'s outside of Utah will pick it up.

Anyway, I was writing to tell you what he was doing as he died. He was writing songs. I know because he called me before he headed home on that flight and he told me. What I didn't know was what he was writing. When the police returned his belongings, they gave me a few scraps of paper along with bits of his guitar and his baseball cap.

I hope you would be so kind as to print these two songs I typed below. It may be the only way the world (or Salt Lake/Provo) will know some of his best work.

Thank you,
James P. D. Bierne
Provo, Utah

Below that letter, printed in the paper, were the lyrics to the last two songs penned by Patrick D. B. Bierne. I will do my best to do them justice:

Sometimes I Forget to Remember

Sometimes I forget to remember
It just seems so much easier that way
If I don't remember
I've got nothin' to say
So I forget to remember every day

Sometimes I forget to remember
The things I did that broke your heart apart
So many to remember
So easy to regret
I just can't remember ... I forget

Sometimes I forget to remember
The things we did together for so long
How your lovin' made me strong
I forget that I was wrong
And I don't remember, on purpose, all day long

Sometimes I forget to remember
The day you said yes, you'd say "I do"
I guess I said so, too
I guess you always knew
I'd forget to remember to be true

One day I'll remember to remember
If I'm man enough, yes, I think I am
I'll remember all your pain
I'll remember to explain
Then maybe you'll forget
And remember
To simply love me one more time again

I hope you liked that ...And now this one ...

The Wind Blows By

The wind blows by
And I think of you
And all those things
You used to do
To make me happy

To make me smile
The wind blows by
I cry a while
The stars come out
And I think of you
The way you promised
To be true
To stand by me
For all my years
Out come the stars
Out come the tears
Sometimes, nothin', nothin' at all
Gets me goin'
And I recall
How you felt
Holding me tight
I got nothin'
I moan all night

The wind blows by
And I think of you
And all those things
You used to do
To make me happy
To make me smile
The wind blows by
I cry a while

And if that was not enough, I give you this final note from the editors at *The Herald*:

NOTE FROM THE EDITOR:
The Daily Herald printed this note from Mr. James P. D. Bierne in its entirety after verifying the facts with the pilot, Mr. Jack Jay, and Mr. Patrick D. B. Bierne's manager,

Mr. Francis Xavier. *The Daily Herald* also confirmed a report from Mr. Xavier that Abington Square Records has signed newcomer Randy Travis to record both of these songs by Mr. Patrick D. B. Bierne.

I for one will remember The Renegades. This is Billy Burke for KSL-TV.

Goodnight and good memories.

####ENDTAPE####

MINE

This is my Saipan,
A battlefield
With no blood,
A soldier
Without a uniform
Fighting the enemy
At close range
Without letup.
This is my Saipan,
Fighting the enemy
Without a gun,
No helmet,
No cover.
This is my Saipan,
Under attack
From the truth,
Bombarded
By large-caliber memories.
This is my Saipan,
Surrounded,
The fight goes on
Far from home
In a remote place,
Unrecognizable.
This is my Saipan,
A place no man should go.
Once there, shattered,
Remembering
The horror,

The smells,
The every days and nights.

This is my Saipan,
An older man
Fighting
To survive
Without proper equipment
Or training,
Alone
On the battlefield.
This my Saipan,
At work
At home
Asleep
Busy
Quiet
Alone
With the past,
Alone
With the future,
No troops,
Just me.
This is my Saipan.
As my father did
In his,
I must survive
In mine.
When do I
Ship home?

LOST KEYS

I lost my keys,
My special ring
With thirty keys
To the things
I need.
I search
For them
Everywhere.
My keys
Are nowhere I look,
I look
In new places.
Nowhere.
When did I see them last?
I have been forgetful
Lately,
Distracted I guess.
I have not
Paid close attention
To my keys.
They will be there
When I need them,
Ready to help me,
But now
They are not.
Not there,
Not here,
Not in my pocket
Close to me,
Not anywhere
I can see.

My keys
Have disappeared,
Thirty keys
On a special ring,
Each one
Permitting me
Access to something.

Without my keys,
I cannot enter,
Cannot start things,
Cannot protect,
Cannot get warm,
Cannot join in.
Where did I put them?
How could I forget
My keys?
All thirty gone,
All at once.
So careless.
Since when?

OPENINGS

Forty-seven first sentences of short stories not yet written

1. THE GOOD MARINE

The leukemia that ravaged his sixty-three-year-old body in less than a year was imported when he was eighteen, following his honorable discharge, following his service to his country, following his obedience, following the footsteps of so many into Nagasaki forty-five days after the bomb.

2. DECADES AND DENIAL

The four boys met in high school forty years ago and had been through a lot together, so the news of the death of one of the men felt more like Russian roulette to the other three.

3. A TALE OF TWO BROTHERS

My older brother and I were born and grew up in Brooklyn; he died at sixty-three, in a hospital on Long Island, twenty-five years before I will likely die in my apartment in New York City, and even though I am past eighty-five now, it is our first fifteen years together that I relive every day.

4. SUNDAYS NOW

A car pulls into the Sunny Way Nursing Home parking lot, and a man too young and physically healthy to really need the cane he uses, walks slowly from the car to the revolving entry door, spinning slowly inside to be greeted by the smells of people who suffer the glory of old age and by the sight of residents dancing with broomsticks or sitting motionless in wheelchairs facing interior walls and as he makes his three-legged way down the attendant-littered hallway to the elevator while deciding who to visit first, his father's mother on the first floor, his mother's mother on the second floor, or his great-aunt, in the worst condition of all, on the third floor, he wonders what floor he will be on, and when.

5. HE WHO ...

He had let so much go that there was almost nothing left to hold onto, and in the presence of gravity, he was experiencing some difficulties.

6. FROM WHERE I SIT ...

Sometimes during Thanksgiving, sometimes, as the phone rings, he can remember, sometimes, the call at Thanksgiving about the football accident, and her youngest brother, Frank, and in his parent's den, he sees football on TV, and through the yellow kitchen wall phone, they hear paralysis reported by long distance from Sienna, NY, to Long Island, in 1980, changing the fabric and trajectory of all their lives, yet the one who handled it with the most grace, then and today, and not sometimes, was Frank.

7. BEHIND EVERY WOMAN

On the outside, the sisters were different, and on the outside, the men they married were different, yet both couples could be seen through the same lens: lucky lovers in a world with few winners.

8. FUN IN ADVERTISING

Stephan had a long and successful career in advertising and ended up sharing ownership of an agency with a milk toast sort of man named Renaldo who had a flamboyant wife named Tennessee and three bookish boys, who did not know, or maybe they did, that Renaldo (Stephan was to discover quite by accident later) liked to dress as a woman at night and sit behind his desk applying too much makeup while having a cup of tea and a smoke.

9. WHERE TO NEXT?

Billy knew his mom loved his dad, but one night he heard his mom ask his dad to please stop gambling on the horses, and please let's join the country club where you can play cards (*and I can keep an eye on you*), and Billy heard it all, even what was in the parentheses.

10. MURDER IN THE MARKEY WOODS

The children emerged from the underground storage tunnel, looked around and saw nothing they recognized; the newly built housing development was gone, replaced by a dairy barn surrounded by open fields and grazing cows, and the only sound they heard was the man with the pitchfork wearing dated clothing and yelling, "Hey you kids, get out of my field."

11. FROM AFAR

July 21, 1917, France

Dearest Kitty, and Mother and Father,

I received your last letter over a week ago and such great news ...I am so sorry for the long delay between letters, but the Captain ordered us to stop while we moved positions and rebuilt our bunkers ...it is not so bad except for being afraid of never seeing you three (four?) again ...can you please send me a picture of Scotty ...I am overjoyed with the news ...

12. A MUCH-NEEDED VACATION

He answered the phone and heard the voice of his wife's tennis
teacher, and he knew immediately what that meant.

13. THE CRITIC

Six year old Billy ran into the sliding glass door at what seemed like a hundred miles per hour; "Wrap his head in a towel and get him in my car," shouted the blind owner of the house.

14. LIFE, OR NOT, IN CONNECTICUT

Little Jack sat in the closet until the arguing stopped, and then he made his move.

15. BETWEEN 9 AND 3

In order to get to the bottom of things, Sister Mary Estelle lined up the boys in front of the blackboard and started to hit the smallest one first with her favorite pointer.

16. THE CEDAR CHEST

The chest sat for years unopened, secrets unrevealed, lives untouched, until tonight.

17. FALLING FOR THE HAMMER

The feeling - no, the recognition - sneaked up on him as he put the key in the door of his rented house, which was three blocks from where his children lived with his ex-wife, and then it hit him right between the eyes as he realized he could commit again, or for the first time, and it was the woman he was dating - yes, her - yes, her, he would commit to her for the rest of his life, and he opened all his closed doors at the same time and felt a rush of warmth and love inside and out.

18. A BOY NAMED FAROUK

The last few weeks were good for Steve, as he was off drugs and doing well in his new job, but without a safety harness, the fall from the ladder caused a host of problems he had never encountered before.

19. MY FIRST CLIENT

Dinner was almost over, and the bill came just as the transvestite show was beginning.

20. A PERFECT DAY

Since the divorce, he had lived in an apartment with a perfect view of the White Horse Tavern, and usually by 11:00 a.m. he could look the other way and have a perfect view of his living room window.

21. GLORY BE?

Father Henry felt his heart stop and wondered about the light that was promised him.

22. THE VISIT

The last joke he remembers his grandfather, Jim, telling was when the doctor told the family Jim had testicular cancer and they would have to remove his testicles ... "Then you better see my wife," Jim said, "She took those years ago."

23. ANTONIO'S BELIEFS

Every day, the shoe polisher, fifty-one-year-old, four-foot eleven-inch Antonio, collected over fifty pairs of shoes from the lockers of the country club members, limping through the locker room on his short leg, smiling and greeting each member by name, his ego steadied by the lift in his own right shoe.

24. HOW THINGS HAPPENED

The two men at the bar stared at each other for what seemed to her a long time, "Make your move," said the older man, and young Betty fell in love right there.

25. REMAINS

The note read: "Have shed my skin ...The gate stopped swinging ...Images attack ...Reconciliation impossible."

26. THE HOLIDAYS

He had figured himself out, and the answers he had been searching so long for were before him now, the raw and twisted truths of his youth revealed all at once, he put the ham in his shopping cart and pushed toward the checkout.

27. THE GIFTED ONES

"I want to have a personality, too," said Bobby as he began the process that would seal his fate.

28. THE RED COAT

It took over five years after his father died to put back on the heavy woolen red winter coat that was his father's first and then his, and then the closet's, and in the pocket were keys to the old house.

29. TRYING TOO HARD

My first wife was a scotch.

30. FOR HIS OWN GOOD

They were all at the bar now, about three rounds in, when his mother used the words "spinal tap" in a sentence; he hadn't heard those two words, in that order, in over thirty years.

31. A WIFE'S CHALLENGE

Henry put the deck down and got up to fetch himself another scotch, he knew his three (imaginary) poker-playing friends needed a few minutes to evaluate the cards they'd been dealt, and he was still thirsty.

32. A MAN, A WOMAN, THREE BOYS

Each Marine in the landing vessel knew they would be hitting the beach at Saipan any second, and with each soldier praying in his own way, the front ramp flopped down, shuddering and splashing and coughing the men into the waiting machine-gun fire, and immediately the spray of bullets killed the five men next to private J. D. before the enemy gunner had to swing the turret in the opposite direction, giving J. D. the moment he needed to live long and lucky enough to marry Norma and have three boys.

33. A BROTHER'S LOVE

"We are not lost, just shut up and hold my hand and keep walking," shouted six year old Phillip to his younger brother, Joseph, but the sound of the cars whizzing by so closely had Joseph doubting his older brother's decision to run away together.

34. TAKE IT OR LEAVE IT

As he lay in bed, Ricky waited nervously to hear his father on the front porch whistling for the family dog, because that sound, like an all-clear siren, meant his dad was sober for the evening in question.

35. AS USUAL

As usual, Nancy walked briskly home from her job as a principal so she could share the rest of the afternoon with her second husband, Tony, who, this day, she discovered dead on their front steps, his keys still in the door, and she immediately thought this departure was nothing like her first husband, John, who left her when their daughter, Mary, was three, and she knew, this time, it would take a while to put her life back together again.

36. THAT WAS A DOOZY

It must have been 101 degrees by now, and the thick insulated gloves made John perspire even more just by looking at them, so up the electrical pole he went gloveless … "Hey, Big John," shouted Jim, his partner, "put 'em on," but John did not have a chance to reply.

37. THANKSGIVING VACATION

The Firebird was moving so fast Richard could not negotiate the hairpin turn, and by the time the car bounced off the rock and hit the telephone pole, his lower lip was already hanging off and in the passenger's seat Peggy was pulling out a Kotex from her purse to help him stop the bleeding and Steve and George, now on top of each other in the backseat, were trying to free themselves from the grip of the crushed interior.

38. APPROACHING EXIT 64

The first time it happened, he was headed home on the same highway he had headed home on for forty years, only this time he felt lost, like a stranger, with no idea which way to go.

39. LETTING GO

The organ music started to play, and he lovingly held his daughter's arm as he escorted her down the aisle, and with each step he saw her change from thirty to birth and back again so fast that his head was spinning, and by the time they reached the altar, he was praying she had learned from his mistakes.

40. SNEAKY PETE

The apartment in New York's Peter Cooper Village was small, so when they put their three-year-old to bed, privacy was never assured.

41. MR. BOB TEACHES GYM

"If I see you with your hands in your pockets, you will feel the back of this paddle," said our new gym teacher, a short, stocky man with powerful-looking arms that seemed to love that idea.

42. TIME WELL SPENT

He was a big shot, seated in the first-class upper bar lounge on the Pan Am flight to Rome for two days of meetings and then back to New York for a screening of his new film—a big shot who had missed three of his daughter's first five birthdays.

43. GOING FOR BROKE

Imagine if you lost all your power.

44. ONE AFTERNOON

There was a small gas leak in the basement of his fiancée's new house, and on the first floor everyone was getting sleepy.

45. AND YE SHALL FIND

The sound could erupt anytime from Kenneth's first grade class desk in the back of the room, or from the first grade class bathroom line, and, sometimes while erupting, Kenneth would punch the lockers, and/or try to bite his tongue, or just flail on the ground as if electrocuted, and the class would just wait motionless, in horror, for the seven to twelve seconds it normally took for the eruption of *"aaaaaaaaaahaaahaaaa"* in a low, guttural monotone to run its epileptic cycle, and this is how James first became aware that feelings of compassion were possible, so how did he forget that lesson?

46. ROADIES

Florida was 1,502 miles away, and the four days it took young Jack to get there with his dad, alone in the 1959 Thunderbird, did not turn out exactly the way Jack had hoped.

47. ANNUNCIATA

She was not a religious woman - superstitious perhaps, cigarette always in hand, her every days were for others - born in Brooklyn, raised in Queens, married to her high school sweetheart, wife to a loving, gambling ex-Marine who broke and mended and broke and mended her heart, mother of three boys who probably did the same, observed by her grandchildren to be a sweet, kind, gentle woman, whose second son held her as she whispered her last words, "Sweet Jesus, where do we go from here?"

OPENINGS

Forty-seven first sentences of short stories not yet written

-THE END-

I FORGOT

I realize
I forgot
To close the shutters
Of my mind

Or left a window
To my heart
Unlocked
Is there a key?
I forgot

Usually
I am sure to keep
All the shades drawn
To my emotions
Drawn tight
And bolt the doors
Of my soul

I think of you
And then
Try to pretend
That I let you in
Did I?
I forgot.

AHEAD?

There is no reconciliation
For the loss,
No antidote
For the confusion,
No anesthesia
For the incomprehension.

Every day
It seems
The water
Is deeper,
Colder,
The shore farther,
The tide stronger.
Every stroke gets harder.

You let it in slowly,
The sharp truth
Like a cancer

Replacing soft, numbing shock,
Shifting the balance
Between weight
And buoyancy.

You cannot move forward
Fully,
So
You move
About,
Sometimes a new step,

Mostly wandering
The territory
Of yesterday,

Trying to reclaim
Time wasted,
Using time
To make time
Come back,

Residing in between
The there
And
The here,
With all the loves here
Mixing
With all the loves there.

The mix has
No gravity,
No oxygen.

You are stalled
But can't be.
You are alive,
Most of you.

Most of you
Needs to move
Ahead?

AT SEE

As a child
He built the boat,
Taught by
His father
To make
It right,
To watch
Over it,
Fix it,
Keep it
Afloat.
Now
Many years
Have passed.
At sea,
The man
In the boat
Rests
In the calm,
Knowing
Calm
Will not last.
He
Is prepared
For the storm
He is sure
Will come.
The man
In the boat
Knows storms.
He rests,

Waiting,
Drifting,
Peacefully
Over the swell,
Prepared,
Waiting,
Drifting
Off
To sleep,
Blind
To the clouds
Blowing in
Over the boat,
Deaf
To the rolling
Thunder
Around the boat,
Rocking
Like a baby
At peace,
Dreaming
For too long,
Unaware
Of the dangers
Surrounding him
And the boat,
Until,
Lightning strikes.
Bolting upright,
Awake,
Surprised
By his neglect,
The man
In the boat
Sees the mast
Fall,
Breaking

The rudder,
And
The rudder
Gouging
The hull.
The hull
His father
Sealed.
The hull
That
Needed attention.
Attention,
Postponed.
The man
In the boat
Tries to fix
The unfixable.
The boat
Takes on water.
The boat
Is sinking.
The man,
Now sinking,
Wonders
How
He missed
The storm,
How he missed
Strengthening
The hull.
The man
Built the boat
With
His father,
Taught to
Care
For the boat,

To love
The boat.
The man
Who missed so much,
Now
Feels the sea
At his knees.
The man
Waits,
The sea
Now
At his shoulders.
Through his tears,
The man
In the boat
Sees
His father.

WHAT I WANT

I want
To be stupid again,
To make mistakes
Without concern,
To act impulsively
Without knowledge of the known,
Callous to consequences,
A brave bastard
When I shouldn't be,
To insult without reason
And more.

Stupid again,
I want to be stupid again,
Alive to enjoy
The time
That is still
Running out.

SHADOW MAN

The shadow man
Slips back
Long ago,
Watching
Himself,
Then
From the shadows
Seeing
All
The mistakes,
The wins,
The rights,
The wrongs.
The shadows
Protect him
From discovery.
He watches
It all
Again,
Discovering
For himself
The world
He knew,
The world
He helped,
The world
He hurt.

The shadows
Protect him
A little now
But do nothing
To help
Those he hurt
Then.

ANOTHER DAY

Another day
Has slipped away.
Where are you?
Where did you go?

Were you here
Just a minute ago?
Maybe hours?
Maybe years?

It's hard to
See the time
Through all these tears.

Where could you be?
Where could you be?

I need you here
Right next to me,

Just like it was,
Like yesterday.

Yet now you are
So far,
So far,
Away.

Where are you now?
Where did you go?
I'll wait for you
Another day.

THE PLACE

There is a place
Between denial
And acknowledgment,
A sliver
Of numbness
Bordered by
The twin insanities
Of
Refusal and reality.
This place
Is reserved
For living
With tragedy.

WHAT WILL THE DAYS SAY?

There is no anymore
There is no ever was
The days gone by
Are gone
The days to come
Ask why
Take your time
They say
We will go away
Were you ever here?
The answer is
What I fear

THE PITCH

WHAT WILL THE

We are in a board room of a movie studio. Several movie executives are sitting around the table awaiting the start of a presentation by Steve and Kevin Kelly. They are twins who are about to pitch their movie idea.

Kevin welcomes and thanks the group, explaining what they are here to do and that they would like funding to produce the idea. Without missing a beat, Steven describes the scene:

"Okay, imagine you are the camera. You are high up in the sky—we are talking a moon vantage point—looking down on the earth, and we are moving in at a steady pace, closer and closer—"

(As Stephen takes a breath, Kevin picks up the description; they are able to go back and forth like this for the rest of the meeting.)

"—and we hear music, holiday music, more like a mix of holiday-style music from many cultures, not just ho-ho-ho stuff, but sitars, guitars, drums, flutes, hands clapping, spoons playing, the Philharmonic ... you get it? Okay—"

"Okay. We hear local sounds from around the world, and we are moving in, and it is the holidays, and we begin to see local cities, mostly small, some big, some very rural locations mixed in with a variety of indigenous cultures. Remember, you are the camera, and you are taking in the scope of the world, so you see many different cultures, some in mountains, some cities, some on plateaus—okay, okay, you get the idea. And you, the camera, keep getting more specific. You see a car bomb, you see a mother giving birth, a handshake, a boy sharpening his bayonet, or a young girl decorating a Christmas tree, or an old man asleep at a bar, or a motorcycle splashing a pedestrian, or a doctor performing battlefield surgery ... and throughout it all, over each scene, you are aware that we are seeing the people saying or thinking just one line. One thought. The lines are connected to tell a story, but the scenes are not linear, and the individuals are edited together to help advance the message, okay? ... So, okay, here goes—remember, you are the camera."

"Stephen and I will alternate the lines and visuals. We are using English here, but the film we be in a variety of languages and subtitled as need be ... okay." "Okay?"

"Okay."

"We call it ... 'Of Everything.'"

"Okay, remember, we pick this up now as the camera has found its way from the long shot, looking at the earth, to closer views of the subjects described ..."

WHAT WE SEE:	WHAT WE HEAR:
(A mother gives birth)	Afraid to make you happy
(Silhouettes watching the sunrise)	Afraid to make you cry
(A smiling man parachutes from a plane)	Afraid to live forever
(A thirteen-year-old boy is behind a sandbag)	Afraid to simply die
(A female student faces her male school principal)	Scared to fail at anything
(A policeman is in pursuit)	Scared to sit and wait
(An elderly man uses a walker to cross the street, no cars about)	Scared to move too quickly
(A sniper takes aim at a convoy)	Scared to hesitate
(A father baths an infant)	Will the water be too cold?
(A wrinkled older woman looks in a mirror)	Will my children grow this old?
(A farmer waits for rain)	Will my day go okay?
(A funeral procession in Bombay)	Will you all go away?
(Lovers watching the moon)	Will night come again?
(A dad slams a door)	Will I regret everything then?
(A grade school boy or girl)	Is it safe to say hi?
(The father of the bride)	Is it safer to cry?

(A finger dialing 911)	Is a minute too long?
(A man signs divorce papers)	Is right sometimes wrong?
(A Head of State giving a speech)	What is real, what is fake?
(A wife next to her husband, staring at the ceiling)	Will I sleep?
(A husband next to his wife, staring at the ceiling)	Will I wake?
(A little girl in a beauty pageant)	Did I love you too much?
(A visiting room in a nursing home, adult kids and ninety-eight-year-old parents)	Did I look but not touch?
(A woman tries on expensive shoes)	Did I take and not give?
(A man punches out at a time clock)	Did I really live?
(A man asleep at a bar)	Afraid of it all
(Father-and-son suicide bombers)	The big and the small
(A tank in a street with protesters)	To act or to freeze?
(A mother holds an infant and scolds a three-year-old)	To anger or please?
(A woman surveys earthquake destruction)	Afraid of it all
(A kitchen scene of domestic violence)	To hang up or to call?
(A local square in the midst of an uprising)	To stand or to fall?
(North and South Korean delegates eyeball each other)	To buzz or to sting?
(A child sees a spider on his hand)	Afraid of everything
(Child stares out the school bus window)	Afraid of all around me
(An artist stares at a blank canvas)	Afraid of what's inside
(Moments before a wedding kiss)	Afraid to stand and take it
(A child in bed in a dark bedroom)	Afraid to run and hide

Kevin and Stephen realize they have finished the storyline but have not prepared an ending suitable to the idea, so Kevin says,

"Any questions so far?"

There is silence, and then from the conference table audience, the twins hear,

"Okay … fine … but how does it end?"

COUNTDOWN.

One hundred nine days
Each one a gift
With the edge of a razor
Cutting into my reality
Reminding me
Of my time
And the lack of his
One hundred nine days
Of confusion
Blending worry and guilt
Hope and the past
With an unknown future
Here I am
For one hundred nine days
Where are you?

Each sixty-three
One sixty-four

You are no longer
In front of me
No longer my scout
Something has happened
In one hundred nine days
I step
On footprintless sand
Fatherless territory
On my own
After all the years
Without you
In just
One hundred nine days
Without you
Even more

THE TRIP INSIDE

This is how it is remembered.
Nothing before.
No discussion remembered.
No cab ride.
Nothing.
After that, the memories begin to begin ...
The boy is on a raised rolling bed with white sheets.
Sitting.
In an outer room.
Windows all around.
Some very vague goodbyes.
A father and a mother and a paper bag leave.
The bag held someone's clothes.
The bed is pushed toward some doors.
The doors are wood.
Pretty.
With glass panels.
Moldings polished.
People are pushing the bed to the doors.
At least two people.
The bed forces the doors open.
Then a hall.
The hall is long and skinny.
Like a hall in an old hospital.
White.
With beds about.
Empty beds.
White sheets.
Down the hall we go.
Left or right?
Into a room.
The room is grayer.

Louder.
Brighter lighting.
More people.
White and blue clothes.
Many strangers.
Not just two.
Lying down now.
Turning or turned over.
Seeing a needle.
Now very scared.
The needle is very long.
Longer than a normal needle.
And thick.
Thicker than a normal needle.
Nurses.
Many nurses.
Six?
The nurses are very strong.
Stronger than normal nurses.
An attack?
Resistance.
More than normal.
Kicking. Screaming.
More of that.
Terror.
More than normal.
Then pain.
The pain is very bad.
Very bad.
More than normal pain.
Then nothing again.
In a minute?
In an hour?
The pain is gone.
The fear inserted.
Silence.
For years.

Silence.
Silence.
The silence hurts more.
And lasts longer.
The act ... misunderstood.
Fifty-five years later.
The pain tempered by time.
The fear thriving
Yet
A misunderstanding.
This act rethought
An act ... of love.
An act ... to protect.
Never discussed.
The attack
Was the silence.
Before, during, after,
Theirs, and mine,
So much time
So quietly wasted.

UNBREAKABLE

Unbreakable
I thought
Uniquely solid
Inside and out
Buoyant with illusions
Fragile as ice

THE BALANCE

My heart ...Is open now
Swinging wide
The door to my soul
Inside a half-filled hole
The loving living
The missing dead
I have a foot on
A threshold
I cannot leave
I miss the missing
Half of my life
Gone
Horrified,
I rejoice now
In the balance

THERE'S A PERSON IN HERE

he could remember a lot not everything because who remembers everything especially after all of the accidents but a lot is good and he remembered a lot that was the lucky part but it was also the unlucky part if he had died he would have been spared the pain of some of those remembrances but he didn't die he was thinking he was just as if frozen in time but he would not trade the painful memories if he could be alive enough to remember the good memories too or at least the memories he thought were good as one thing he knew now was that his recollections may or may not be true to what actually really happened but he does remember stuff so that's what he's got the stuff he remembers as he remembers it and now the way it is he has no contradictions so he can does might make stuff up in a way that pleases him or hurts him depending on the subject like his family or getting fired from a job for the wrong reasons or hurting his wife wives kids others or his childhood especially his childhood because those memories were affected long ago by many things long before the injury or at least long before *this* injury because there were others weren't there yes there were there are always injuries to the brain but not through the head usually the injuries to the brain are through the heart but it doesn't matter because they are really painful just the same so he does remember a lot and it is the quality and shape of those memories that is somewhat random let's take one he thinks of remembering from the backseat of the car parked at the shopping center the woman nervously lighting a cigarette crying softly about money and diamonds at Christmas and love hurting more and remembering matching glasses of VO and an argument with a somebody like his father about Nixon and Vietnam that is pretty vivid for him a couch a man a VO and an argument with a teenager about life death right wrong a man who had been a fighter and a boy who never was arguing about the value of war and the right to kill but then the memory shifts to the draft and the details of waking up and worrying about the lottery in 1971 and the risk of actually going over there and the phone call from his father this is clear get up he said read the *New York Times* or not but get up he said and go drop your deferment and get the loop hole so he remembers he thanked Melvin Laird and he did what he was told to do like he usually did only he liked it this time that he remembers now still in here with voices heard through the memories of the draft board man asking him if he was sure and he said yes and signed and waited three months for the year to end and he remembers that night too when he was in the clear and wouldn't die in Vietnam but he didn't know then that he might die so many ways and the memories now of the cancer and the memory of forgetting the cancer ring so true he's not making *those* up no how could he because he was never that creative sure he could twist things like raising his kids too loudly yelling yes really yelling by twisting that to discipline in a good for them way but not full-blown out of the blue made up stuff anyway not like the way he hid the cancer from everyone including himself even after the operation for so long it was like dying in Vietnam anyway but he didn't die anywhere not even from drinking too much and passing out on the edge of a pond he just got sick but he forgets that because who cares but he remembers a lot like being married too early lying in the grass the day before that moment and asking whwywhwywhy and never having an answer until too late but he remembers asking but he just forgot the answer but did he or not and that was just the first marriage he remembers in detail all three births from that misguided union the births that were guided directly to his heart to hold dear and kept him alive after the divorce he remembers that ok and he remembers lying in the apartment and willing it to end it all but not taking action because he remembered a lot about why he was alive not for him now but for them and that came with a price he remembers the thoughts of that but not the price so on it went and on and throughout many ons and ons and offs he recalls more off days than on days but hiding the off ones behind a smile a drink or twelve to stay *on* for thirty years of *on while off* but who cares is that another memory he is creating or not he did it anyway it being the money the advertising jobs the family the Marines like winning he remembered his dad doing so he remembers modeling himself after his dad but like a bad Xerox the fine details missing just an image similar to the desired one and remembering he was afraid that he forgot all of

171

this yet he could remember a lot now lying here for how long *that* he could not remember because he did not know before and you can't remember something you never knew or could you well he did not know the answer or answers and needed to rest but never could never did all his life except hung-over then he rested but that's not really rest but now he needed a rest from the injury and the sixty years of self-inflicted glory and damage but could not rest would not rest as he was remembering all the time moving in the memories which was exhausting as he moved so far over distance time emotion so fast and remembering too much or not enough was hard work for him as his brain and ears worked but not much else which was ironic he thought because *before* the injury those were the only two parts of him people complained about him didn't work he remembered that without laughter because he could not laugh like this and what was there beyond that irony to laugh at so he remembered funny things to see if that helped but every funny thing memory went by too fast shadowed by other types sad types and or death type memories mostly not good ones but a few understandable ones most unbelievable and he remembered a lot about a lot of these and like he could not laugh for the fleeting funny ones he could not cry for these bad ones now not now not like this but then after so many years of not crying he did cry for so long and at so many odd times but not now not like this yet he remembered the crying and he remembered the first death he knew at four upstairs in a grandmother's house the man with the cane who hit the floor to get attention was resting now cane in the closet resting too and the stairs smelled like something other than his grandmother's cooking and he left that house and he remembers those people and stories in bits and pieces like puzzles from different boxes that somehow fit together in the memories he had or made up and he remembers Winnie the forty-five year old best friend of his great aunt and he remembers Winnie's head shaking uncontrollably on her forty-five year old body he remembers Aunt Kitty forty-five and Winnie at lunch Winnie's head shaking and hand waving smiling happily to a 1958 camera and finding this picture thirty years later in a cedar chest that held so many other memories photos from holidays Saipan weddings communions and things bayonets and WWI discharge papers and report cards and hair and dried flowers and lives gone by he remembers the mingling of fifty years of keepsakes in the cedar chest he sneaked into and used to form his thoughts his always to be hidden history just waiting in the basement's cedar chest and he remembers one small picture is from a boat going overseas to France and more where he knows now he would go with his new wife before they were married but when they worked together and it was wet and cold there but they were warm together then married and the memories explode in his mind about the fluctuating temperature of his second marriage that despite variations kept him warmer than now here after all this warmest now remembering the birth of his second son her only one and then wanting to remain warm reminding him to remember the redcoated man watching a dog and a boy and a hill and sleds and screaming and thirsty with two brothers then always and now to fifty years later holidays as a family quieter than when younger and together then and now too few times a year but still together he remembers how it was then loyalties times three remembering how good loyalties felt and now he remembers and he remembers a door to his life he thought then she saved him his second wife did she was the door that opened him up helped him through what needed helping through like his brothers helped him stood by him like that he remembers like that and sleeps for a few minutes or hours or how long he never knows how long things take now he just remembers how long things are gone which seems always now like forever but how could they be really gone if he can remember and the remembering is now then the memories are now and then can be now for an instant or longer or shorter he could not tell about time now it was all so confusing a dog a bike a hill the injury all mix in moments mixing so lying on the ground deciding whether or not to get married at twenty-one is in the same year as the birth of his three grandchildren which spanned five years but felt like today or at once but was thirty years later which was how it all stirred in his mind the dates and invisible timelines that read like the cosmopolitan notebook he wrote in in catholic school at six or rolled all together like weed in college too much bunched together in a joint and it just made him sick sometimes so he didn't smoke and effortlessly put most of those memories in a box where his heart shouldn't be either remembering when he was nine sitting on the curb in the rain thinking about what it would be like when he was older more grown up than now about how many kids he would have what kind of father he would be compared to his father what kind of husband he would be while he was waiting for his grandparents to show up from Boston where they lived to visit his family over Christmas with presents and butterscotch brownies that he liked a lot in the cold a long time waiting out of his house away from his mother and father who he called mom and dad never by their names that he never would use his whole life until after they died in 1988 but he didn't even know that in 1958 along with his dog he waited since he hung up the phone with his grandparents when they said they were just leaving Boston and would be there soon so out he went to meet them not dressed warm enough because it was cold where he sat for hours until a blue Oldsmobile turned left onto the street where he waited for two people he loved and had fun with his whole life until when he was forty they died but not before they showed up so he stopped thinking about growing older worrying about how he would turn out worrying about the courage he would have or not have to live a life without regrets true to himself so when he died he could say just before it happened it's okay because he was true to himself whoever that was to him only not being able to realize the futility of that wish a wish made futile by all that had come before together with all that would arrive later in life which somehow he was able to see clearly even though it was freezing cold they were shouting hello he was nine his dog was barking and it was dark especially on his street where nights were long and noisy almost every night except when his grandparents would arrive from Boston calming the usual routine down so he could relax enough to be himself whoever that was which didn't often happen then or for the next thirty years of his life until he opened his eyes for a year to what had happened to him around him in him closing him up making him feel like for thirty years he had been sitting waiting on the curb in the cold waiting for love to make a left turn onto the freezing icy street of his mind not even realizing he had closed that street to all cars except one that came was not acknowledged stayed a while and then left accidentally dented adding even more dents to the frame so accidentally damaged in past accidents by those even more careless than he and the silence of that remembering was interrupted by the sounds of beeps he thinks beeps and now he thinks there was always beeping in this place he is but not that he cared to notice as he remembered things a lot of things and the beeps and words he remembers blended to a hum at times the blending and memories running over the hum breaking through the hum like it was then and he could hear his daughter call for him when she fell off her bike at five and he dropped his coffee yelled for his first wife then and took their second child mouth bleeding to the dentist and she was okay he remembers the weather then as cold fall cold and the Polaroid from the dentist's office is lost now but he remembers her face the face he loves and she is thirty-five now and the face he sees is all ages all her faces that helped then and help now sustain him and he remembers when he as the boy he simply dropped the Oreo into the ivy next to the sidewalk and he as the boy simply watched in amazement as his father reached down scooped up the cookie and ate it smiling at his son with a that's how it's done bravado and of course the memory is real of him the boy staring at this man this father this hero wondering if he too would no could be that brave and the memories of wondering are endless and the truth of the bravery achieved remembered to different degrees now as better or worse depending he guesses on what he chooses to remember at least that is how it feels to him now and here from this angle of nothingness and his daughters still love him he remembers because they said so after all he did and didn't do and he remembers all the faces of all his children and more and his first daughter with her head held high loving him and he even surprises himself to remember his father enlisted in the Marines at seventeen years old head held high too and so young to face a war away from home or better than the war at home and he remembered always wondering about that wondering too how parents fear the death of a child and remembering in horror remembering a son who helped others not himself too giving too alive to live and he shook and shook and beepbeepbeeps went faster and sometimes he knew it was true and he sometimes remembered it might not be which was not often but usually worked if he remembered he had grandchildren from his firstborn elder daughter three grandchildren to remember and that is better yes better than death he remembered births births births births and one gone he misses now but these births of his from him he cherished then beeps and hums and pain he remembers a lot all the time from all the times and all the times remind him of other times including skiing with his five-year old first son teaching him to ski a little down the mountain to be grabbed and then do it again until his son turned left on his own which he could do well and went past him fast and went until his son tumbled over and now that son is gone from the mountain and gone for too long forever actually from here and from everywhere actually and he remembers how but not why and the place his first son is now is unvisitable in person and still the beeps beep and he wants now to listen hard to the beeps to forget his son's passing and the details he knows in detail and that he remembers a lot even at times he does not want to remember so he tries to remember other things in advance creating memories in advance his advance memories that he would have had if those he knew had not died yet had lived and this fills him for a few moments with a false happiness based on false memories of false times with true loved ones so many loved ones to choose to play his game son father mother grandparents best friend wife of best friend coworkers childhood friends soon maybe even himself and the beeps keep pace with his memory of names and places a cadence now created and propelling him through time and stories he remembers these things as he remembers to try to move and can't or blink and can't so he remembers a lot and can't communicate to anyone but himself which at least he enjoys most of the time but not always depending on what he thinks he thinks and how long this goes on he can't remember but there is plenty of time to remember a communion white shirts young and older men cold Rheingold beer a fist fight falling from a tree breaking a wrist watching caskets parading through the years so many he had what could be called season tickets at his church and drinking bouts shouting bouts car crashes and Christmases all colliding in a timeswirl that is his head on something he cannot feel maybe a pillow or shirts in a drawer maybe a casket no too noisy to be dead he thinks and thinks and thinks and thinks yes he is alive in a way still alive and the hollow part of him is still breathing not like his first son but thank god like his other three children thank god thank you what God he thinks he is right he remembers them alive three of them but he has not seen them since all of this happened or heard a single voice other than all the dead voices that he allows himself to hear wanting so much to hear the living especially the living he was like this before he remembers maybe not exactly but he remembers lying out flat not able to move like now but it was then he was held down but he remembers not moving just the same when the long needle went in his spine and he remembers the fear that went into his spine with that needle and how the fear became a part of him even when the needle was not but slowly drew out the fluid to see if he had meningitis he remembers he did not have meningitis polio or anything else wrong with him you could see until cancer way later but what he got from that needle visit was not so good either he remembers trips to the hospital for births and deaths too so he tries to remember births and sees his fourth child first and remembers details and hospital memories of his second son so beautiful and handsome smiling as if to say *yes yes yes I am here and it is impossible but we did it you me ma all together* and with this he remembers his first daughter's head rising after delivery in the delivery room to look around the room head held high and head held high all her life and his second daughter's umbilical cord wrapped around her neck which held up her beautiful first face turning blue fast so he flipped the cord off and she turned healthy not the other way around like his first son he remembers cutting the cord of his first son that day but not knowing then that his third child would unknowingly cut the cord on himself thirty years later and how now he cannot will not cut any cords now or ever with his own first son not ever no matter what happened which was so bad but he can't cut it out of himself and he won't even try though that departure was more painful and horrific than the spinal tap when he was four or a life of spinal taps for that matter or when he was whatever and he remembers when he was twenty thirty forty he did not remember like this but approaching sixty four now now he remembers it was as if he remembered nothing knew nothing learned nothing from his past but boxed it sealed it buried it and remembered to forget it so now he remembers now oh he remembers so much now how much damage he caused and he estimates it was a lot spread all around like a cancer and he is not sure he can undo it even though he wants to undo so much then he remembers he wants to redo so much too so he just remembers what he can remember and tries to rest again which is impossible and why rest when there is so much he can remember like a time long ago on a hill out back a sunny day when he was uncorrupted blank open to interpretations a time when light was knowledge not exposure a time when warm meant close not pain and cold was unknown except when touching now a half century later he feels it again it is then again he lives or tries to live uncorrupted remembering this through and for and through his children all four of them chambers of his heart beating for him in him with him in the memory of then and now and later breaking through the disasters misunderstandings retreats breakdowns to an in-between space that is easier to navigate now than any day he remembers even though he remembers an injury and not moving he remembers to stay curious to try always try always trying to remember to be the person he could be the person inside to open the drawer he imagined he was in or really was in and get out of there and stand up and walk out front pause and bow remembering a job well done he remembers he was at his very best so rarely so fleetingly and surprisingly he remembers this and now he sees his adult children's faces ahead of him now but not now but twenty years ahead of him but before him in twenty years or thirty and he remembers in advance how he will be there waiting will they see him will they remember please remember he says he will be there always in front of them inside them beside them a hand outstretched as if he could be asking for the pleasure of their company he remembers so much and he wants to remember it all even though he is not moving and colder now he remembers there is a person in here remembering and this person wants to remember it all

EPILOGUE

And a man came to a place he had been before
A long time ago
A place of originality
Of belonging
As if he was meant to be there
As if he had always been there
But he knew now he had left
And was back

ABOUT THE AUTHOR

James Patrick has won industry awards both as an advertising executive and a filmmaker.

He is a colon cancer survivor, a not so award winning husband, the father of four children, a mourner of one adult child, a grandfather of three, the brother of two men, a relative to many, a friend to some, and much less to others.

In 2012, he re-thought everything, re-energized his acting career, and has completed several feature films. Born in 1950, in Peter Cooper Village, New York, he has been working on this memoir for over 60 years.

CPSIA information can be obtained
at www.ICGtesting.com
Printed in the USA
LVHW042325301121
704796LV00004B/103